Yorkshire

Edited By Donna Samworth

First published in Great Britain in 2018 by:

Young Writers
Remus House
Coltsfoot Drive
Peterborough
PE2 9BF
Telephone: 01733 890066
Website: www.youngwriters.co.uk

FOREWORD

Young Writers was created in 1991 with the express purpose of promoting and encouraging creative writing. Each competition we create is tailored to the relevant age group, hopefully giving each child the inspiration and incentive to create their own piece of work, whether it's a poem or a short story. We truly believe that seeing their work in print gives pupils a sense of achievement and pride in their work and themselves.

Every day children bring their toys to life, creating fantastic worlds and exciting adventures, using nothing more than the power of their imagination. What better subject then for primary school pupils to write about, capturing these ideas in a mini saga – a story of just 100 words. With so few words to work with, these young writers have really had to consider their words carefully, honing their writing skills so that every word counts towards creating a complete story.

Within these pages you will find stories about toys coming to life when we're not looking and tales of peril when toys go missing or get lost! Some young writers went even further into the idea of play and imagination, and you may find magical lands or fantastic adventures as they explore their creativity. Each one showcases the talent of these budding new writers as they learn the skills of writing, and we hope you are as entertained by them as we are.

CONTENTS

Reuben Turner (10)	60	Robert Dylan Coates (10)	102
Amelia Hartshorne (9)	61		
Ruby Ella Welsh (10)	62		
Aminah Akhtar (10)	63		

Keelham Primary School, Bradford

Ellie Marie Chalmers (10)	64	Alex Mark Ludbrook (7)	103
Bobbi Elizabeth Scaife-Wheatley (10)	65	Theo-Cole Cyprien (8)	104
Jessica Innocent (9)	66	Zack Charles Elliott (8)	105
Nabeel Baig (10)	67	Courtney Mannion (8)	106
Moeez Hussain (10)	68	Radhika Parmar (7)	107
Ibrahim Ashfaq (9)	69	Lucy Jacques	108
Evie Grace Hebbron (9)	70	Holden Roberts (8)	109
Charlie Waterhouse (9)	71	Scarlett Ava Simkiss (8)	110
Olivia Dobson (9)	72	Muhammad Hamzah (7)	111
Laila Shaher (9)	73	Emily Walter (7)	112
Kaitlyn Gage (10)	74	Pearl Roberts (7)	113
Eshan Bashir (9)	75	Charlie Michael Carter (8)	114
Aleena Ahmed (9)	76	Ethan Holroyd (7)	115
Duaa Farooq (9)	77	Travis Mark Tailford (7)	116
Daisy Armitage (9)	78	Lili Runaviciute	117
Isaac Morrison Lee (9)	79	Molly-May Thornton (8)	118
Haseeb Shah (9)	80	Ellie Drake (8)	119
Aamnah Adris (9)	81	Bethany Wood (8)	120

Zidan Nawaz (9) — 82

Sana Mohammed (9) — 83

Mill Lane Junior Infant & Early Years School, Batley

Isaak Patterson (9)	84		
Ellie Keenan (10)	85	Ayesha Sheraz (9)	121
Hayat Malik (9)	86	Zara Ali (10)	122
Soheeb Mahmood (9)	87	Adetutu Eniola (11)	123
Max Usher (9)	88	Rumaan Anwary (11)	124
Zayyan Altaf (9)	89	Haniyah Maqbool (10)	125
Eliza Din (9)	90	Jabeer Mohammed (10)	126
Aliya Din (9)	91	Dominic Powles (10)	127
Jesse Jay French (10)	92	Zulaika Laher (10)	128
Thomas Williams (9)	93	Aleeza Khan (11)	129
Lilly May Davies (9)	94	Zara Mahmood (11)	130
Devon Anne Garbutt (10)	95	Huzaifah Seedat (10)	131
Iman Malik (9)	96	Codi Slocombe (10)	132
Zakariyya Rafi (9)	97	Jorja Bedford (10)	133
Amani Mariam Fardin (10)	98	Hafsa Hussain (10)	134
Fatimah Ali (9)	99	Evie-Mai Gott (9)	135
Ella Armstrong (9)	100	Zainab Mahmood (10)	136
Murtaza Ishfaq (10)	101	Salma Hussain (9)	137

Kaif Zanfar (10)	138
Selina Ashiq (10)	139
Umaimah Hussain (10)	140
Fahad Raja (10)	141
Nathan Wagner (10)	142

Totley All Saints CE Primary School, Sheffield

Daisy Snowden	143
Lily Hope Naylor (11)	144
Aron King (11)	145
Jessica Smith (11)	146
Lily Pearl Flint (11)	147
Rafi Jack Day (11)	148

Woodley SEN School & College, Huddersfield

Kyle Hanson (10)	149
Logan Watt (11)	150
Tyler O'Donnell (10)	151
Charlie Green (12)	152
Thomas Dunning (12)	153
Max Jagger (12)	154
Rudie Hughes (12)	155
Brandon Johnson (12)	156

Beijing The Town's Trickster

The clock struck twelve. The innocent victim couldn't fall asleep. She didn't know she was being watched by the doll, Beijing, which lay beside her toy box.

Once she'd fallen asleep, Beijing crept over to the bed and whispered, "She's asleep!" The toys rose up from where they soundlessly lay. "Hide under the bed!" commanded the doll and they obeyed. The queer doll raised her hand. *Tap. Tap.* The tapping grew louder. The human-shaped figure woke up, frightened. Several heads popped from under the bed.

"Ahhh!" screamed the girl.

"I knew it would work!" cackled the doll.

Tayyiba Nafees (8)
Barkerend Academy, Pollard Park

Charlotte The Doll's Wonderful Hairstyles

Charlotte was the toy box's best hairstyler. Her owner, Stephanie, on the other hand, was awful! She'd come back from school and ruin her beautiful dolls.
One day, her mother called her for dinner. "Coming!" shouted Stephanie and left the room. "Ah!" came a little voice, "just enough time to fix my hair!" It was Charlotte. She rose from the floor and hopped to the mirror. In thirty seconds, her hair was so pretty, your eyeballs would've popped out! "She's coming!" exclaimed Charlotte. She hopped back to her place and stayed still. Stephanie was impressed with her new hairstyle.

Mariam Ahmed
Barkerend Academy, Pollard Park

The Head Of The Army

"To infinity and beyond!" shouted Buzz, "I've scanned the area and it seems Woody's hat isn't in the room. It looks like we have to take this downstairs."

"Aye, aye Sergeant, move out!" exclaimed Chief Soldier. They slowly climbed down the creaking steps until they had, at last, reached the bottom. Suddenly, they heard the cry of their worst enemy, the vacuum. On hearing that, they hid behind the chair. "No!" cried Chief as one of his men had been sucked up. Then, the chair was pushed away. "Andy, you have left your toys here! Oh, it's Woody's hat!"

Shabbeer Ali (11)
Barkerend Academy, Pollard Park

Fugitoy The Cleverest Of All

Late last night, as the wind was howling, Fugitoy, who was the cleverest toy in the world, said, "Is the car fixed because we need to go to Toys 'R' Us?" "No!" screamed Josh, the monster. So clever, brave Fugitoy fixed the vehicle and drove it to Toys 'R' Us. The triceratops tried to blow up the vehicle but Fugitoy drove back to the road.

Everybody got scared because the triceratops horribly said, "What are your last words? You are going to die!" As fast as a cheetah, Fugitoy crashed the triceratops. *Kaboom! Bang!*

Everyone screamed, "We are safe!"

Yahya Hussain (9)

Barkerend Academy, Pollard Park

The Slimester

"Slimy, now's the time, let's go," whispered Slime 1. With the slimester asleep, they knew what had to be done. As the slime squelched over the floor, the slimester snored. The door creaked open and they quietly shifted themselves out of the room. "Quickly, make it to the bathroom so we can exit!" said Slimy. They quickly made it to the bathroom. *Squelch! Squelch!* Stanley heard and quickly approached the bathroom. "Ssh, someone is coming!" whispered Slimy. Stanley opened the door and stared, wondering why his toys were here. He took everyone and dumped them into the cupboard.

Urooj Karim (10)

Barkerend Academy, Pollard Park

Magical Dream Of Pigs

Max was asleep. The toy pigs wanted to explore the room; they wanted to see the other toys. Pong, the leader, was directing where to go. They leapt over Max's phone on the floor and saw mud on his boots. It made a squelch. Max was awake. Max inquired, "Why are you here?"
They replied, "Sorry."
Max giggled, "Just kidding!" Max was playing with them. He went to get some water. He stepped on a pig. *Oink!* Max woke up from his sleep.
His mum came in. Mum asked, "What happened?"
He replied, "I just had the best dream ever!"

Sharif Uddin

Barkerend Academy, Pollard Park

The Fidget Spinner

Three minions jumped out of a toy box. Bob walked over to a fidget spinner, he stood on the pad. Stuart followed and started spinning it. Kevin hopped on. "Weee!" Kevin let go and went flying! He smashed into a wall. *Whoosh!* Kevin landed between two blades. His body split in half and he died. Bob and Stuart screamed.

"Ahhh!" Bob cried. Slowly, Kevin's body slid back into position.

Then, Ella woke up, stood up and squished something flat. "Huh?" Ella said. She looked down to her minions, squished in a pile like some tangled wires. "Oh, no!"

Anisa Ahmed (11)

Barkerend Academy, Pollard Park

Untitled

Late last night, the princess said, "Oh, I'm going to bed!" Then, the creepy toys crept into the room. She said, "Oh, what's happening to me? Am I going to die?"
The goblin said, "No! You're not." The princess got really scared, worried and terrified. When the moon was full, the Power Ranger toys came alive. They grew. They went on their super motorcycle and rescued her. But not quite because there were some Basher Bots in the way. They had to destroy them, then, the goblin. At last, they destroyed him and got her home. They became small again.

Jakia Hussain (8)
Barkerend Academy, Pollard Park

Tiddle's Big Birthday

One late night, inside Sam's house, it was time to go to bed. The only thing he didn't know about his bedroom was that his toys were alive! When Sam wasn't playing with his toys, they jumped about! Tiddle was a bear. It was his birthday but he didn't know it. His friend, Tiger, was planning a party. "Come on toys, it's Tiddle's birthday!" Tiddle was hungry. He went to the kitchen to get honey but the cat was there!

"Oh no! It's the monster!" Then, he snuck outside. "Surprise!" said Tiger. Tiddle had the best birthday ever!

Aisha Najabat Hussain (8)
Barkerend Academy, Pollard Park

Freedom

Waking up from her deep sleep, Lavopa woke up her friends and told them to get ready to leave. Her friends immediately got up and got ready. They were walking on their tiptoes so that the humans wouldn't hear a noise.

Minutes later, they had reached the door and they had trouble opening it. They eventually managed to open it. Lavopa and her friends were so close to escaping when a human walked past! They froze. Thankfully, the human never noticed them.

By the time they reached the door, it was 10, so they rushed outside and closed the door.

Aqdas Jahangir (11)
Barkerend Academy, Pollard Park

Revenge

It was time. The day where Ross would finally get to hang out with his friend, Jeff, once again after a long time. He had missed Jeff but he was taken by the toy army force because he had been accused of stealing a unicorn. He was framed by his enemy, Pete. However, Jeff had sworn revenge and promised that he would get back at Pete.

In the afternoon, Ross went to pick up Jeff. Jeff ran to Ross and told him, "Now is our chance!" as he pointed towards Pete.

"It's time for revenge, let's get him," Ross said.

Junaid Ahmad (10)
Barkerend Academy, Pollard Park

Robot Invasion

The clock struck midnight. Robot toys came to life. As soon as their invasion started, humans tried to stop them. The robots started their attack. The army of robots worked as brave as knights. The boss of the robots shouted commands to all of his little minions. The courageous robots fought with their little pea shooters until there was nothing but human blood.

After their victory, they held a party with other toys. Behind them came a shadow. It was a human figure. He got out a weapon and in no time, every single toy was gone!

Muhammad Salih Ijaz (11)

Barkerend Academy, Pollard Park

OggBogg's Doom

Once upon a time, there was a toy dinosaur named OggBogg. He lived with his friends, happily. One day, his friends noticed that the batteries were running low. "OggBogg, your battery is running low!" OggBogg made a shiny smile, knowing his batteries would die. The toys crept towards the door and towered up to open it and ran. They found the toolbox and opened it. They swam in the tools and eventually found the batteries they needed. The toys ran back to the room and fixed the batteries into dead OggBogg. "Hurray!"

Mohammed Shuayb Fahim Ahmed (10)
Barkerend Academy, Pollard Park

Princess Amy

Once upon a time, there lived a toy king and queen. They had a baby named Princess Amy. Princess Amy was a lovely, adorable doll with big blue eyes and golden-yellow hair. She grew up to be a wonderful young lady.

One day, Princess Amy decided she would go to her favourite part of the castle which was the garden. In the garden, there were lots of different flowers. Princess Amy loved roses the most.

One day, Princess Amy saw a prince walking in the rose garden. The prince saw Amy and fell in love with her so they married.

Hadiyah Hussain (10)
Barkerend Academy, Pollard Park

Me And My Rabbit

One dark night, I was awoken by a noise. I couldn't think what the noise could be. I was staring at the ceiling which was as bright as the moonlight. It was coming through the curtains. I heard whispering, "Play with me!" I looked under my bed and I saw my old, rusty rabbit toy. He was moving by himself. I grabbed him with my bare hands and started to dance in the moonlight. The rabbit was singing loudly. The old toys started too. We danced all night until daylight. The rabbit and old toys were happy and thankful.

Nimrah Asif (9)

Barkerend Academy, Pollard Park

Quick! We're Late!

One early morning, me and Spike shouted, "We got VIP tickets to a concert!"
They all shouted, "Yeah!" They got up from their beds. Me and Spike shouted,
"We're late!" So we got up and set off as fast as we could. Well, I guess we were the only ones going somewhere.
"We're late," said Horsee, "come on my back, we'll go faster then!" So we all went on his back.
"Finally, we made it!" said the baby tiger. We relaxed and watched the show!

Umarah Begum (9)
Barkerend Academy, Pollard Park

The Princess Who Fought

A toy princess named Clare had always had a dream about becoming a princess who could fight. She went to school and found a friend who was not a princess. Clare invited her over for a cup of tea.

When they got to her house, her father told the princess that he fights for the freedom of the world. Clare was so interested that she and her friend went with him to fight.

They fought and fought until they won. The princess' father was so impressed that he told her she could fight because she was a brilliant fighter.

Humairaa Sideeqah (10)
Barkerend Academy, Pollard Park

Tim's Favourite Toy

It was Tim's birthday and it was time to open his presents. Most of his presents were dull and boring and not to his interest. Mum saw the sadness on Tim's face so a few days later, she surprised him with a megasaurus! He had sharp claws like fangs and had a mane like a lion. He had a loud roar that frightened the other toys, except Tim. The other toys decided to frame the megasaurus in order to get rid of him. Surprisingly, they put themselves in danger and the megasaurus was the hero who saved them!

Mohammad Huzaifah (10)
Barkerend Academy, Pollard Park

The Hidden World!

The night before Daniel had gone to bed, he had been playing with his little toy car. In the middle of the night, he heard some noises on the window. He got up and saw his toy car had turned into a real car! The car said, "Daniel, let's go!" All of a sudden, Daniel was in the car, driving above the sky. There were thousands of other toys alive. Daniel was gobsmacked! All of the toys had started to talk to him. They all started to play. He went back home. "Daniel, time for school!" shouted Mum.

Zayed Rahman (10)
Barkerend Academy, Pollard Park

Toys Are Helpless!

Once upon a time, there was a stretchy thing named Squishy. He was a hero. If you heard the toy news, this all began when a teddy, soldier and alien were playing on a ceiling fan. The game they were playing was 'Who Falls Off?'.
Minutes later, a human came in! He turned on the ceiling fan and ran off! Just then, Squishy saw them in danger and sprang himself to the wall. He stretched himself to the top of the wall. The little lizard made a turn. He stretched towards the fan and saved the little toys.

Rifa Afrin Miah (10)
Barkerend Academy, Pollard Park

The Lonely Eed Teddy

Once there was a little teddy called Eed. He had wanted to be a teddy in the fantastic, friendly teddy village but actually, the teddies were not friendly. They were spreading rumours. Eed did not like the village, he wanted to go home.

One day, he decided to go the Olympics. He started to swim. He was nervous at first but guess what? He actually won the medal! He was very proud of himself.

When he got back to the village, all the bears said, "Sorry!" Eed accepted their apologies.

Maria Hoque (8)

Barkerend Academy, Pollard Park

The Teddy Who Eats All The Cookies

Once there was a toy factory that made all sorts of toys. One day, they thought a teddy was made wrong and they were going to throw it away. All the boys went to the shop. Everyone wanted it! The teddy's now owned by a five-year-old boy.

The teddy slept under the bed. Every night, it came alive when nobody was awake. His guards were always on the lookout when the teddy stole cookies for a picnic.

One night, he got cookies but he got caught by his owner. He quickly turned into a statue.

Sallis Shah (11)
Barkerend Academy, Pollard Park

The Great Escape

Molly the doll had been placed on a shelf so people would buy her. It had been years in the store and she'd planned an escape. She told her friends about the escape when the store was about to close. It was 8pm. Molly and her friends snuck up to the exit door and because they were small, the people would not see them.

Yay! They had escaped! In Molly's doll's house, they had a party all night. They were the happiest toys ever! Then, she woke up! She was dreaming the whole time!

Thaiba Hussain (10)

Barkerend Academy, Pollard Park

The Night Of The Living Toys

At midnight, everyone was asleep in their bed, cuddled up. Suddenly, a cute-looking doll became alive, as well as the other toys! After that, the toys threw a party. At their party, they had cake, balloons, party games and much more! The toys had a lot of fun at the enjoyable party. The party was as fun as a birthday party in a fun place like Alphabet Zoo or places like that.

Finally, the party was finished so all the toys began to tidy up. After that, all the toys went back to their toy boxes.

Sana Fatima
Barkerend Academy, Pollard Park

The Lonely Car

Joe had just bought a new toy car, he was super excited. It was night-time so Joe had to sleep. He couldn't wait for tomorrow. Joe fell asleep and the toy car started to explore around the house. The car was really excited because it never had a friend before. Suddenly, Joe heard a sound which woke him up. The toy car rushed to the same spot where Joe had slept. Joe ignored the sound and went back to sleep.

The next day, Joe happily woke up and played with his car. It was the best day ever.

Akil Miah (11)

Barkerend Academy, Pollard Park

The Slaying Robot

Once upon a time, there was Robot Land and there was the bravest and strongest boy called Manuel Never and he was a slaying robot. Manuel Never was bullied by his next-door neighbours and his friends, who were now not Manuel Never's friends. His friends went to a and some people bought his friends in Toys 'R' Us. Manuel Never went to Toys 'R' Us because he missed his friends, even though they were bullying him. He ran until he got to Toys 'R' Us and saved his friends.

Abdulaziz Ali (8)
Barkerend Academy, Pollard Park

The Lost Barbie

One day, Lilly was playing with her doll, Chloe. What Lilly didn't know was, all her toys could come to life!

On Wednesday, her friend came over and played with her dolly. When it was time for her friend to leave, her friend took the doll with her. When Lilly went back upstairs to play, her doll was not there! Her doll was looking for her everywhere but she couldn't find her. Chloe then saw her in the ice cream parlour and ran towards her and froze. Lilly burst into tears of joy.

Hafsah Massood Hussain (10)
Barkerend Academy, Pollard Park

Untitled

One gloomy Thursday morning, Barbie and Chelsea were in the living room, very hungry. "I'm hungry and could eat a pizza!" said Barbie. They quickly climbed out of the toy box and ran to the kitchen. First, they climbed onto the kitchen table but they fell down. Next, they climbed on the chair and got the pizza out of the fridge. Then, Barbie put it in the oven. Finally, they ate the pizza. "This is tasty!" said Chelsea. They went to play with their friends.

Hiba Hussain (8)
Barkerend Academy, Pollard Park

The Lost Horn

Once there was a pony. A robot, who was turned bad by an elf, stole her horn. She decided that now was the time to get it back! She saw the robot put it in a chest and lock it. Then, she saw the robot put the key in a safe.

At night, when the robot had a rest, she sneakily got it and opened the chest but it was the wrong key! So, she asked the soldiers to fight the robot so they did. Peach got the key and opened the chest. She finally had her horn back!

Afsana Bibi
Barkerend Academy, Pollard Park

The Jolly Runaway

Far, far away, in a magical land, there lived a toy owl with a girl. They lived in a mansion. The girl loved the owl so she took it out everywhere she went. Then, one sunny day, she was eating lunch and her owl saw the window and dashed for it as quick as he could. Then, the girl finished her lunch and saw her owl had gone! Every single day, she would cry and cry. Suddenly, the owl flew back in her face and she was relieved. From that day on, she had a toy owl.

Haneefa Ahmed (8)
Barkerend Academy, Pollard Park

The Evil Witch

Once upon a time, there lived a nasty witch who cursed a precious toy. The witch had only cursed part of it. Sometimes it was bad, sometimes it was good. The toy was sent to destroy the world. Tom, the owner of the pet, didn't know about this until that night. He watched the toy go to the witch. He knew it was cursed. He read a book on how to save the toy and killed the witch. Tom quickly put the potion in the toy and it was saved!

Al-Sami Miah (10)
Barkerend Academy, Pollard Park

Untitled

One dark night, a big, fat toy appeared. It was Big-Fat-Bum! They lived in a closet. Big-Fat-Bum and his terrible army planned to go shopping. So, they got a trolley, a book and a human mask. They were about to go but the shopping alert rang so the toys gave their owner payback. They stuffed the toilet with tissue but someone accidentally pressed the flush button! *Clash!* They were trying to swim but they drowned. How watery.

Yasaa Uddin (8)
Barkerend Academy, Pollard Park

The Adventures Of The Toys

Once upon a time, there was a toy whose name was Buzz Lightyear. People didn't know it was coming out for sale until a boy called Tom was crossing the street. He saw the toy, he wanted it so he went into the shop. He was the only one there. The toy cost so much but luckily Tom had money so he bought it.

When Tom was coming home, his mean neighbour made fun of him. Tom ignored him and went to play with his toy.

Sumayah Khanum (8)
Barkerend Academy, Pollard Park

Big Ben Bear And His Army!

"Ben," whispered Patch, "let's go!"
"Okay!" whispered Ben.
As they got out, one by one they tiptoed to the staircase. Ben was leading the teddy bear army as they went down the staircase. Suddenly, they could see the huge party down the bottom of the staircase. "Quickly, get up the staircase!" said Ben, trying to push everyone up. "Humans, humans!" he cried. "Forget about the cake! Get back up!" Everyone was back up the staircase. "Phew! No one caught us! Now, let's go to sleep! Oh, look! We have some cake!" said Ben.
"Yay!" everybody cheered.

Ronald Sedgwick (8)
Carr Junior School, Acomb

Untitled

One day in February, a little girl named Kate was playing with her toys when she realised what time it was. She was late for school! As the large oak door slammed shut, Cozmo awoke. "She's gone. Time to explore!" whispered Cozmo as he wandered off.

Half an hour later, as Cozmo was climbing the stairs, he heard a thud. "Oh, no! Dog!" yelled Cozmo as he spun away after the dog hit him in the legs. Suddenly, Cozmo heard Kate's voice. "No!" He ran back to the chair that was covered in fluff.

"I'm home, Cozmo!" shouted Kate.

Katie Innes (9)

Carr Junior School, Acomb

The Magical Tale Of Unicorns

Esmé the unicorn was going to a party and all of her friends were going to come in a prom dress but Esmé was not. Esmé was wearing a summer dress. Also, she felt left out because she was wearing a summer dress and everybody else was wearing a dress and high heels. But Esmé was not wearing high heels, Esmé was wearing dolly shoes. Esmé thought that all of her friends would make fun of her because she was wearing flats and all of her friends were wearing high heels for the party. However, the party was amazing.

Cara-Jean Margaret Ethel Chittock (9)
Carr Junior School, Acomb

Little Bird Needs A Home

One sunny day, a beautiful toy baby bird woke up from a deep sleep. The bird was hoping that she'd wake up in her room but she didn't. She was lost! "Oh, no!" cried the bird, "I'm scared!" She started by going to other houses to see if she could find her family. "That kind of worked," said the bird, "I'll never find my family," she said. Her family were going on a walk and saw her.
They asked, "Are you our daughter?"
The bird said, "I think I am!"
So they all went home and lived together.

Julia Irena Semczyszyn (9)
Carr Junior School, Acomb

Emelie's Freaky Foot

In a normal house, down an ordinary street, under an extraordinary single bed, lived a toy princess, Emelie, and her family. Whilst Emelie was popular, two nasty toys called Maggie and Florence had a cunning plan to banish Emelie from the toy box. They were so mean.

One day, they tripped Emelie and because she was made of plastic, her foot came off! Disaster had struck! She was now a hazardous toy! The mission was on to fix her and never, ever allow a human to see.

A few hours later, her foot was perfectly fine. They had succeeded!

Emily Hughes (9)
Carr Junior School, Acomb

Bye-Bye Dr Pineapple

One bright, sunny day, a sweet girl called Emily was just about to go to the park. She said bye to her favourite toy, Dr Pineapple, then she slammed the door and left. Then, Dr Pineapple started to party with his best friend, Patch! Suddenly, they heard the door slam. Dr Pineapple was so worried. When Emily opened the door, Dr Pineapple shouted, "Hi, Emily! Welcome back!" Emily screamed so loud, Emily's mum's ears popped and she came running as fast as she could. They were so scared, they sold Dr Pineapple to a girl named Hayley.

Lucy Skidmore (10)
Carr Junior School, Acomb

Will They Get Home Again?

Once upon a time, there was a big . Princess Unicorn Sparkles a.k.a PUS and her friends woke up as the guard closed up for the night. All of the toys gathered round and they had a vibrant party. Surprisingly, something appeared on the floor. "What is this?" Barbie said in a squeaky voice. "I think that is a portal!" exclaimed PUS. They pressed the button and shot off and landed on a rainbow! They slid down and realised that they were on a desert island! Everyone thought, *will we get home again?*

Isabel Harriss (10)
Carr Junior School, Acomb

Blobby's Adventure

Once upon a time, there was a huge monster teddy that belonged to Toby. He called the monster Blobby.

Over time, Toby forgot about Blobby somehow and he ended up at the back of the room where the toys that he didn't want went, in the bin! Blobby woke up and said, "Where am I?" He jumped out of the rubbish truck and found himself at the park at midnight. Suddenly, he started walking and found a humongous river. He swam gracefully across the river. On the other side was his house, he was relieved!

Caitlin Summer Bagley (9)
Carr Junior School, Acomb

Pearl And The Great Adventure

As I took a tiny step towards the peephole, I saw my opponent, Darkblade. He was there and I was in my box. My life had been ripped to shreds by him! His warriors were called Grey-Blades, they were as tough as me and my friends. We jumped from our boxes and leapt across the room, towards a ruby. Sadly, Darkblade saw and stopped us. One of his warriors caught the ruby. Barbie squirted him with her hand and brought it to me. I thanked her and we jumped back into our boxes and held them ever so tightly.

Emelia Stead (9)
Carr Junior School, Acomb

The Toys That Escape

When I went to school at 9 o'clock, I heard
something coming from my room. I thought it was
my toys but I just carried on walking. Then, I saw
one of my toys walking out of my house! It was
Jackson, my favourite teddy! He had glasses and
a green top and a pair of blue jeans. Then, I saw
lots of my toys! I saw Cruise, my bright gold car,
carrying a cake in her gold roof! Then, I saw
Jackson, my all-time favourite bear. *Wow, I never
knew that toys could come to life.*

Noah Towey (8)
Carr Junior School, Acomb

A Day Which Changed Candy's Life

Bored out of her mind, Candy stared blankly at the clock. Seconds felt like minutes, minutes felt like hours. All at once, Candy was carried into what looked like a shadowy cave. The hollow filled with chilly water as bubbles rose. Fluid slowly seeped through her skin as the immense chamber began to spin violently like a tornado until she closed her eyes and wished it would stop. Surprisingly, Candy woke up and her eyes opened. She realised she was back, tucked up in her bed, all warm and cosy and smelling of luxurious roses. *What a bizarre adventure!*

Emma Rose Skerrett (9)
Cottingham Croxby Primary School, Hull

The Shape Toy!

One day, a boy called Bobby was walking slowly around the park. All the other toys were shaking in laughter at him! Bobby, who had enough of the other toys being rude, came up to them and said, "I'm not funny! I'm made of shapes and that's that!" He stomped off. Bobby walked on and on and then suddenly, he fell off the Earth and landed on Jupiter. On Jupiter, there was a big asteroid storm! Bobby found a place to live and settled in. A thousand years later, Bobby is still living on Jupiter. Bobby likes it there.

Charlie Langdale (9)
Cottingham Croxby Primary School, Hull

Daisy The Daring Doll

There once was a doll called Daisy. She lived in a castle in a toyshop in Spain. She wanted to be a knight. One night, a huge dragon attacked the castle. The flames scared the knights away. Who would save the castle and toyshop now? Daisy said she would save the day, every toy laughed because she was a girl. Daisy had an idea! She would dress as a knight and scare the dragon off.

Daisy attacked the dragon with her knight's sword. That scared the dragon off. All of the other toys were shocked it was the girl, Daisy!

Daisy Grace Whelan (8)
Cottingham Croxby Primary School, Hull

The Slime

Some slime was made for a toy but the slime was different to all the other slimes! This slime was alive! It was put into a doll so it wouldn't break as easily but the slime took over the doll and it could walk.

At night, in a girl's room, she had a plan to escape because the slime wanted to explore the world. The slime needed to get to the plastic bag, climb the books and jump out the window. So she did her plan and it was a big success. Now, she has gone to explore the world!

Finley Swanson (10)
Cottingham Croxby Primary School, Hull

Labyrinth

"Time to go to sleep," said Mum.
"But I want to play with my toys!" said Jimmy.
"Spike was made leader!"
"Go to sleep now!"
"Fine!"
"Toys, let's steal! He's asleep!" whispered Spike.
Suddenly, the toys were puzzled. "Where are we?"
The gang looked around. All they could see were
paths. It looked like a maze.
"Surprise! You are in an abandoned factory. Let's
see if you can escape!"
They were searching for hours, looking for an exit,
until they spotted a hatch.
"We're free!" The gang opened the hatch and
escaped and got home safely.
"Nooo!" shouted the voice.

Mustafaa Ifzal (10)
Green Lane Primary Academy, Middlesbrough

Penelope's Party

"Stop bouncing on the bed, she's coming!" said Penelope the doll, as a little girl walked into the room.

"I'm back!" she yelled and hugged her toys.

Her mum called from downstairs, "Teatime!"

"Okay," Imogen replied, as she skipped out of her big room.

"She's gone!" Penelope whispered, and carried on bouncing on Imogen's bed. Then, Penelope and her friends went into Imogen's doll's house, where Penelope lived. Imogen came back into her room, and couldn't find her toys anywhere! "How strange." Suddenly, Imogen heard a strange noise coming from her doll's house. It sounded like a really good party!

Matilda Davis (9)

Green Lane Primary Academy, Middlesbrough

Cozmo's Christmas

"Santa, Cozmo's ready!" shouted the elf.
"Great, wrap him, ready for delivery!" replied Santa.
Cozmo was a very intelligent robot who could do lots of things. Cozmo felt nervous about getting a new owner. He worried he wouldn't get played with. Before Cozmo could ask Santa who he was getting delivered to, an elf wrapped him up and put him onto the sleigh. Santa delivered Cozmo to Elliot's house. Cozmo waited all night until Elliot opened him.
Elliot said, "This is the best toy ever! I'll play with him every day!" Cozmo thought, *I'm the luckiest toy in the world!*

Elliot Brynn (9)
Green Lane Primary Academy, Middlesbrough

Unicorn Troubles

"I have lots of troubles! Oh! My back is killing me!" said the rocking unicorn. "All because she's been on my back for ages." The unicorn was getting moody.

"Wait until you hear what happened to me!" said the Lalaloopsy.

"I know what happened to you, I was in the same room as you, remember?"

"Oh yeah!"

"Chill out!" said Barbie, who sat beside the designer friend. The toys always had little arguments. Every time at eight o'clock the toys came to life. "Hah!"

"What happened here? You're alive!" cried the little girl, Berry. "Argh! Mummy, Daddy! They're alive!"

Hiba Brahimi (9)
Green Lane Primary Academy, Middlesbrough

Lego Ninjago

Garmadon arrived in his massive machine, the Garmatron. It was fierce, menacing and powerful, crashing everything in its path. Garmadon drove his undefeatable weapon of colossal power whilst his toy cannon fired dark matter missiles at Ninjago. Immediately Kia, Jay, Lloyd, Zain and Cole came and attempted to stop Garmadon. Kai's fire mech was called in for burning all of the skeleton army, whilst Zain's water mech propelled humongous blasts of water at the Garmatron. The rest screamed, "You shall never destroy Ninjago!" and eventually, Zain's water pulses destroyed the Garmatron and they all yelled, "Never!" and started to celebrate.

Joe Kaafar (9)
Green Lane Primary Academy, Middlesbrough

The Toy Box

I opened my eyes and saw pitch-black. "Where are we?" said Mrs Potato Head.
"I think we're in a toy box," I said. As I looked around, I saw a light. Suddenly, I pushed the roof off the toy box and we all jumped out of it.
"We're in Kate's room!" said Teddy. I looked around and the window was open.
"We can escape through there!" I said. "Quick! Before Kate gets home!"
We all heard footsteps.
"Quick!" cried Teddy.
"Hurry!" shouted Mrs Potato Head. Kate opened the door, but we were gone as quick as a flash!
"Phew, that was close!"

Paige Wilson (10)
Green Lane Primary Academy, Middlesbrough

A Superhero's Story

Bang! Splash! A thunderstorm started. "Could my day get any worse?" mumbled the muscular superhero. "Left outside in the dark after saving the world! I need to get inside!" He climbed out from beneath the trampoline, grabbed a leaf for cover, quickly ran, jumped over pebbles and dodged thorns. "Thank goodness for that!" Sprinting through the cold kitchen, he squeezed under the door and headed towards the stairs. The stairs were gigantic! After scaling the last step, suddenly, a light shone through a crack in the door. Timmy emerged! "Quick, freeze!"
"How did you get in here?" questioned Timmy.

Chloe Richardson (10)
Green Lane Primary Academy, Middlesbrough

Toy Story

Early morning on a sunny day, Andy opened the curtains and left for school.
All the toys came to life, walking towards the middle of the room.
Mr Potato Head said, "Morning honey!"
Mrs Potato Head replies, "Morning!"
Woody shouted, "Buuuzz! Buuuzz!" Silence!
Everyone looked around, under the bed in the drawers. "Look, Buzz! in the car!" shouted Rex.
They all ran to the car. Woody led the way! The door was open.
"Run!" screamed Ham! As they reached the car, they saw Buzz dancing!
Buzz opened the car door, "Come on in! Dance to the music!" Everyone partied.

Zain Hamza (9)
Green Lane Primary Academy, Middlesbrough

The Collar Mystery

One mischievous night, Porky the evil pig crept into the toy palace, unnoticed.
Felicity Whiskers was sleeping in her magical bed. Porky crept into the queen's bedroom and stole the prized collar.
The next morning, Queen Cat woke up and screamed, "Argh!" The collar has disappeared. She rushed to the garden and assigned her dog, Buster, a secret mission to find the collar. Buster sprinted to Porky's castle. Eventually, he arrived, crept into Porky's room, and found lots of stolen items, including the collar! Quietly, he picked it up and escaped. He returned the prized collar to Felicity, who was overjoyed.

Evie Bruin (9)

Green Lane Primary Academy, Middlesbrough

The Doll

There was a knock on the door. "Can you answer it please Katie?"
Unexpectedly, she was met by a mysterious looking doll, what happened next was beyond belief! "Hello, my name is Ellie!" The doll could speak, Katie and her partner, David, were pleasantly surprised by this.
From that day on, they both developed an inseparable bond with Ellie. As time passed, the doll began to deteriorate. The couple rushed to find some replacement batteries, but to no avail, Ellie was slowly fading away. She managed to mutter one final word. "Goodbye!" She then turned off and stopped functioning completely.

Khadijah Nazir (9)
Green Lane Primary Academy, Middlesbrough

The Missing Springs

"Simone Sheep is counting!" shouted Springy Dog. They all rushed to find a hiding spot. Springy Dog hid behind a chest of drawers.

"Here I come, ready or not!" shouted Simone. Springy Dog giggled, "Ha, ha, ha!"

"Ssh!" shushed Tony Turtle who was also hiding behind the drawers.

"Found you!" cried Simone. As Springy Dog waddled out, some of his springs fell out and he fell apart.

"Ow! Look at my springs!" he shouted. The friends gathered to find the springs and then Lilly found them under the chest of drawers. They all put Springy Dog back together.

Jodieleigh Smith (9)
Green Lane Primary Academy, Middlesbrough

Peter's Escape

"Help!" shouted the toy, "seriously again!" Peter the figure was stuck in his owner's garden, all alone. "I'm a prince, I'm supposed to be saving the love of my life!" exclaimed Peter. He had nothing to do, so he grabbed a long stick and began to draw out his return plan. "The window is my only option," sighed Peter.

He climbed up the pipe, trying to pull himself up, except doing the total opposite and dragging himself down. He eventually got there in time, before the girl began to play with her toy figures. "Mr Prince!" giggled the little girl.

Rania Majid (10)
Green Lane Primary Academy, Middlesbrough

Lotso Finds A Smell

"I wish I didn't need to eat strawberries to smell like strawberries," groaned Lotso the bear. "They're horrid!" Off he went to explore a new smell. He travelled to a greengrocer's shop in hope of discovering a better smell. Lotso tried a variety of fruits, such as apples, pears and oranges but his favourite fruit was banana, so he ate a banana, but he didn't like the taste anymore.

Luckily, there was a chocolate fondue in the corner of the shop. Lotso thought, *why not?* and dipped in a strawberry. "Strawberries are not so bad after all!" exclaimed Lotso.

Reuben Turner (10)

Green Lane Primary Academy, Middlesbrough

Untitled

Swiftly running, eight-year-old Eddy climbed the steep stairs like a wild monkey with his frizzy ginger hair flowing behind him. "Do not run up and down the stairs Ed! You will fall!"
"Okay, Mom! Alex, I'm home!" Alex was his favourite teddy of all! Suddenly, Katy the golden retriever jumped past Eddy and burst into his room. She was excited to see Alex. "No!" shouted Eddy, but it was too late...
"Ouch!" wailed Alex the bear. This was the moment now, his fate was doomed.
Katy's sharp, dangerous teeth sunk deeply into his dark, shiny, soft fur coat.

Amelia Hartshorne (9)
Green Lane Primary Academy, Middlesbrough

Jessie In Disneyland

"Psst! Jessie!" Woody, the toy cowboy, quietly whispered. "Are we there yet?"
"No, fifteen more minutes!" Jessie said as they heard a funny noise, it was a voice.
"Fasten your seatbelts! We are going to land!" The door opened. They ran down the stairs, and as they got a taxi, they looked around. They got to the hotel room and dumped their bags. They headed to the theme park. They ran to the Minnie Mouse Castle, then the Goofy Coaster.
"I love all the rides! Woohoo!" Jessie cried.
"Meee tooo!" shouted Woody.

Ruby Ella Welsh (10)
Green Lane Primary Academy, Middlesbrough

Teddy Gave Hope

The earthquake had left fear, children had been separated from their parents. Katy sat with her eyes filled with tears, clutching her teddy bear tight. "Where's my mummy?" she cried, there was no answer. Katy looked hard at the teddy, it belonged to her.

She pushed it's chest for it to say, "I love you!" She hugged the teddy tighter and fell asleep.

She was suddenly woken up by a familiar voice. It was her father, "Jane, I found her!" Katy jumped in his arms and felt a gentle squeeze from her mother. It was a relief they'd been reunited.

Aminah Akhtar (10)

Green Lane Primary Academy, Middlesbrough

Just In Time

The terror in Stinky Dog's face was clear as his 'friends' lifted him up and carried him towards the stain. "No, please!" he cried, "Emily will know I've moved, I can't get back up!"
"Who cares," laughed Jerry.
Moments later, Stinky found himself at the bottom of the stairs. In an act of panic, he tried to climb up the first step but failed. Everyone came down to try and heave him up. "We can do it!" said Silly Sally, out of breath. The second they got to the top, they heard the door open...
They had just made it!

Ellie Marie Chalmers (10)
Green Lane Primary Academy, Middlesbrough

My Strange Rag Doll

A dark winter's afternoon, a bolt of lightning struck the class window. "It's only the weather," Miss said, "let's get your toys and sit down." Olivia was missing but her toy was on the mat, moving on its own!

Lola said, "Look, Miss! The doll is dancing!"

"Help me!" Olivia popped out of the doll and said, "What an adventure we've just had! The doll sucked me in when the lightning struck but where it took me was amazing, like another world! All the toys were alive, should I tell you about it?"

"Okay!"

Bobbi Elizabeth Scaife-Wheatley (10)

Green Lane Primary Academy, Middlesbrough

A Christmas Surprise

Whilst Jack was peacefully dreaming on Christmas Eve, an extraordinary thing happened, a tiny shiny silver UFO flew through his open bedroom window and crashed onto his rug. "How will we get back to the mothership?" cried Alien Zig.
"Maybe someone here will help?" replied Alien Zog, It was at that exact moment, Jack awoke to discover his 'present' from Santa! Imagine his surprise when he picked up his new toy to play with it and two tiny green men from a planet far away tumbled out. Jack truly believed all of his Christmases had come at once.

Jessica Innocent (9)
Green Lane Primary Academy, Middlesbrough

A Robot Who Destroyed Christmas

On Christmas Eve, in the North Pole, the little elves were busy packing Christmas gifts.

On a dark, cold, winter night, the shiny, silver robot came to life to destroy Christmas once and for all. The mysterious robot had planned to take over Christmas. The robot burst out of its packaging and went over to Santa's sleigh. It started to point its laser at the presents in the sack to leave the children without Christmas presents. As it damaged Santa's sleigh, it heard loud footsteps. It was Santa who had called his elves. "The robot is trying to destroy Christmas!"

Nabeel Baig (10)
Green Lane Primary Academy, Middlesbrough

The Giant Robot

"Everyone hide! It's coming!" All eyes glued to it, as it moved to grab its next prey. The claw opened and captured poor Ted. Everyone watched in shock as it lifted him away. *Clang!* Ted dropped back, and everyone sighed in relief but knew that was not the last of demogorgan. Something had to be done, so they helped! Next time it was ready to attack, they had to stop it once and for all.
"Ready, set, go!"
They tied its claws together so it could not capture anyone else. Finally, it was defeated. "Well done, team!" said Ted, happily.

Moeez Hussain (10)

Green Lane Primary Academy, Middlesbrough

Untitled

"Sir, I've got good news, I've looked around the area and the coast is clear! But keep alert because Andy and his parents are coming back. That's all Sir," said the green army toy soldier, marching back to the rest of the soldiers. The enemy was knocked out.

"Let's move!" said the commander, "Now, down the rope and activate Operation Dynamo!" Hundreds of men slid down and some parachuted from the loft. They all picked up one toy each but there was one toy, it was the biggest and the best toy, so five men lifted it carefully upstairs.

Ibrahim Ashfaq (9)
Green Lane Primary Academy, Middlesbrough

Crockersville

Melinda the toy unicorn was anxious. She had no idea where she was. She had been taken from a Christmas Fair and she was brought to a strange place. She could hear other toys talking about Crockersville and what a magical place it was. She was taken upstairs by a little boy and placed onto his bed. When the boy left, she looked around and saw the bed had transformed into a fantastic town, full of toys! She looked curiously as a stuffed crocodile smiled and said, "Welcome to Crockersville! I'm the mayor!"
Melinda smiled and said, "I'm home!"

Evie Grace Hebbron (9)
Green Lane Primary Academy, Middlesbrough

Chapter One: The Bunny Who Saved All

In Lego Bunny Village, Little William, the prince bunny, has been kidnapped by the evil sorcerer, White Tiger and his sidekick, Red Ted. Big William, the great bunny, sets off to find him at Crew Gorge, but then he sees Red Ted guarding the gate. Big William snaps Red Ted's neck clean off with the great blade of Exodia. As he smashes the gate down he sees White Tiger throwing Little William into Volcano of Lego. "Stop!" shouts Big William. He pushes White Tiger into the volcano, where he perishes. William pulls William out and they return to Bunny Village.

Charlie Waterhouse (9)
Green Lane Primary Academy, Middlesbrough

Tinsel's Wonderful Adventure

Tinsel the elf worked in Santa's workshop. She and the other elves helped Santa make all the toys and presents. After a long day, toy making, Tinsel fell asleep in Santa's sleigh, not realising it was Christmas Eve. She was woken by a jingling noise and cold air blowing in her face. While she was sleeping, the sleigh had been filled with presents which had covered her. Santa turned around to take a present from the sleigh and saw Tinsel among the presents.
Santa gave a loud laugh and asked her to help deliver the presents.
What a wonderful adventure!

Olivia Dobson (9)
Green Lane Primary Academy, Middlesbrough

Lily The Unicorn

One day my parents decided to go to Carlton Bank. I went into the forest. Something sparkly caught my eye. "Wow!" A toy unicorn! There was a note attached to it.

"Come on, Laila, time to go home!" shouted Dad. Once home, I got out the note: 'Please look after Lily, she's magical'.

"Wow!" I got out Lily's sparkles and threw them on the wall. I saw a beautiful forest, full of unicorns running around. This is where Lily came from. The years passed and I returned Lily to Carlton Bank for someone else to enjoy.

Laila Shaher (9)
Green Lane Primary Academy, Middlesbrough

A Day In The Life Of A Newborn's Toy

The day has come. I have finally been bought from the shop! It's 9am and I get to meet my newborn human soon. As I happily leave the shop, I shout, "Goodbye fellow friends, my destiny awaits!" Unfortunately, my destiny turns out to be a snoozefest. The newborn won't wake up! Finally, at 1pm he awakes. What does he do? He is sick on me! A forty-five minutes terrifying washing machine cycle is not my destiny! It's 6pm and I'm losing hope of bonding with this human, but then, he turns his little face, and he smiles. It's amazing!

Kaitlyn Gage (10)
Green Lane Primary Academy, Middlesbrough

My Best Friend Is A Robot

The shop fell dark, the door slammed shut, I shouted, "Wait!" but it was too late.
If only I hadn't tripped over the football! I might have made it out. *Maybe it won't be so bad after all*, I thought. A shop full of toys to myself!
"Hello," a voice said, red eyes staring. I looked in amazement at the robot. "Jump on!" he called, as he whizzed by on a remote-controlled car. He was too fast, So I grabbed a bike and chased behind excitedly. I woke up, startled by all the customers. Was it all a dream?

Eshan Bashir (9)
Green Lane Primary Academy, Middlesbrough

Buzz Bear Experiences Candy Land

Buzz Bear lived in a toy store. One day, Buzz Bear's boss sent him on an important quest in Candy Land. When Buzz Bear arrived, he saw tons of candy.

He pushed through the sticky strawberry laces, the fluffy candyfloss, he bounced over the soft, squishy gummy bear. Buzz Bear swept past the tall, solid, strong-scented candy cane, he wriggled past the fruit chews that were bursting with flavour. Buzz Bear swooped over the sherbet flying saucers, Buzz Bear looked up. He saw a luminous light that shone on the last obstacle.

Could he get past the obstacle?

Aleena Ahmed (9)
Green Lane Primary Academy, Middlesbrough

Duaa And The Grizzly Bear

I wandered away, without knowing where my mum was. I shouted, "Mum, where are you?" I whispered to myself, "This store is gigantic, how did I end up in the bear section?" Unexpectedly, the bears have come to life and they are surrounding me. I yelled, "Help me! They're alive!" I ran as fast as I could and slipped on the hard surface of the store. I tried to get up, but the bears were on top of me holding me down! I felt my shoulders shake, I woke up. I couldn't believe that I was dreaming this whole time.

Duaa Farooq (9)
Green Lane Primary Academy, Middlesbrough

The Bear Who Did Not Sleep

Stan didn't go to sleep. Every night he would squirm about in a bed.

One night, when Tilly woke up, Stan was on the floor. "Argh! Not Stan again," she said.

The next day, Tilly thought hard about how she was going to keep Stan in bed.

She couldn't concentrate at school for thinking of ways to keep him asleep.

She decided that she would hug him tighter and keep him on the other side of the bed.

That night, she put her plan into action. Guess what, it worked. He stayed asleep all night and every night since then.

Daisy Armitage (9)

Green Lane Primary Academy, Middlesbrough

The Midnight Beast

It all started in a pitch-black room at midnight.
There was a teddy, Boro Bear, in bed, cuddled up
with a boy named George. He checked that he was
asleep, and tiptoed out of bed. He sneaked
downstairs. His midnight adventure started!
Boro Bear climbs up the drawers to the biscuit tin.
He grabs five Oreos. He met up with his friends,
Chelsea Bear and Arsenal Bear. They accidentally
spilt Cheerios on the floor. "Oh no!" cried Chelsea
Bear. The bears creep upstairs and go into the
Mum and Dad's room. They find some boxes...

Isaac Morrison Lee (9)
Green Lane Primary Academy, Middlesbrough

The Ugly Monster

Tim's favourite toy was Super Soldier. His enemy was Ugly Monster. Tim would make them battle every day, and Super Soldier would win every time! Super Soldier, once again, was bashing Ugly Monster. The monster fell off the table and broke his arm. Tim threw him into the bin. Ugly Monster was sad. He never wanted to be evil. Now, he would never be a hero. Billy, Tim's younger brother, saw the broken toy. He picked up the monster. Billy fixed the toy with a toy robot arm. Now, Ugly Monster became Super Robo Beast, Billy's favourite hero!

Haseeb Shah (9)

Green Lane Primary Academy, Middlesbrough

The Magical Toyshop

Aamnah just came back from the magical toyshop. Mummy had bought her a doll for her birthday. Soft plastic hands and feet, with long yellow hair. Aamnah played and slept with it every day. Little did we know that Rapunzel was a magic doll. When she was alone with her toy friends, they all came alive, they could talk, walk and do everything.

One day, Aamnah broke her leg and lost Rapunzel on the way to the hospital.

Four days later, no sign of Rapunzel, Aamnah felt disappointed. Aamnah found Rapunzel and was so happy. She loved Rapunzel!

Aamnah Adris (9)

Green Lane Primary Academy, Middlesbrough

Billy Saves The Day

Every day at midnight, the toy store comes to life, all the toys play with each other. At the back of the store, a toy named Billy, the blue monkey, causes havoc with his mischievous behaviour. All the other toys avoid him because of his silliness. One day, Billy noticed that the back door had been broken! He tried to alert all the other toys but they avoided him. The cheeky monkey grabbed hold of Mr Hammer and smashed the alert button, which terrified the robbers who quickly ran out of the toy store. After this, everybody liked crazy Billy.

Zidan Nawaz (9)
Green Lane Primary Academy, Middlesbrough

Bell's Mysterious Toys!

A little girl named Bell loves to play in her magical bedroom and she also loves to play with her toys, especially with her favourite doll Millie that she got for her second birthday. But what do the toys do when Bell leaves the room, and when she's not playing with them?. Suddenly, the toys magically come to life and start talking to each other!.Then, the toys overhear Bell's mum talking about this brand new Barbie doll that she's going to get for Bell's sixth birthday. Is she ever going to play with any of her old toys again?

Sana Mohammed (9)

Green Lane Primary Academy, Middlesbrough

Aero's Adventure

Aero dreamed of going to France because he wanted to go on an adventure but there was a problem. The problem was getting out of the toy factory. One day, somebody came and bought him. He saw that it was his chance to escape! He took off. "Here I come, France!" As he flew across the sea, he started to stop. "I'm going to land in the sea, ahhhh!" *Splash!* Luckily, he floated as a fisherman was passing by. He was saved because the fisherman was bringing him back home, to France! "Hooray! I am going to France!"

Isaak Patterson (9)
Green Lane Primary Academy, Middlesbrough

Itchy, Scratchy And The Dragon

Itchy and Scratchy, the toy figures went to the old toy castle. They went inside.

As they crept through the dark passage, in the shadows was a figure sleeping in a corner. Itchy went to have a closer look and saw it was a three-headed dragon. They looked around and every step they took, they shivered with fright.

Scratchy said, "I think we should get out of here!" Just at that moment, they heard a loud yawn and the dragon was awoken. Itchy and Scratchy ran with the dragon running and roaring fire behind them both.

Ellie Keenan (10)

Green Lane Primary Academy, Middlesbrough

New House

The winding staircase leading to the attic was ahead. As I got to the top, the crooked door unlatched and opened on its own accord. There sat a great wardrobe which was meticulously carved. It looked as if it had sat there for centuries, undisturbed. As I crossed the room, I passed many usual objects which had gathered dust over many years. Turning the heavy brass knob, there sat a porcelain doll. The doll appeared innocent enough, however, it had a sinister presence which unnerved me. Its stare was piercing as it looked into my soul...

Hayat Malik (9)
Green Lane Primary Academy, Middlesbrough

The Evil Santa

One day, in a land not far away, there was an evil Santa who used to take all the children's toys! One day, near Christmas, the evil Santa went to Tom's house. Tom was a seven-year-old boy who loved to see Santa. The Santa said, "I've come to take your toys, ha, ha, ha!"

Tom said to the evil Santa, "You should give toys to children and say merry Christmas, ho, ho, ho!" Tom had a plan. He tricked the evil Santa by telling him the toys were in the cellar! When Santa went down, Tom locked the door.

Soheeb Mahmood (9)
Green Lane Primary Academy, Middlesbrough

Mason The Helper (Christmas Addition)

A loud noise came from downstairs, Mason the teddy bear woke up. He jumped off Max's bed, past the two dogs on the landing, down the stairs to the front room where he saw Santa. Santa was on the floor all tangled up in the Christmas tree lights with presents scattered all over the floor. Mason straight away began to help Santa take off the lights and put the presents back into his large black sack. When they finished, Santa thanked Mason for his help, winked, smiled, then disappeared up the chimney in a sooty cloud of smoke.

Max Usher (9)
Green Lane Primary Academy, Middlesbrough

The Great Ninja Escape

Early in the morning, I was playing with my favourite toy Lego. I love to play with it, but one night, when I was asleep my Lego figures came to life!

The general was called Kai, he was a good guy. His enemy was awake and had captured the other ninjas. He knew what to do! He went to Kruncha Fortress. It was heavily guarded. The general had a sword and knocked the guards out! Kruncha was going to turn them evil with the ultimate weapon. Kai grabbed it first and saved his friends from destruction. Kai was a hero!

Zayyan Altaf (9)

Green Lane Primary Academy, Middlesbrough

A Living Doll Named Angelina

One day in Sophie's room, she was playing dolls with her friend, Rosie. Sophie decided to pick her favourite doll who was called Angelina. Rosie had her own doll called Samantha. Sophie lent another doll to her but she said, "It's okay, Sophie, I have Samantha with me!" But just as Rosie said that Angelina started to move.

As the days went on, Sophie was having more and more fun. Sophie adored Angelina. Angelina turned back to a doll, but Sophie didn't mind, at least she had a little bit of fun!

Eliza Din (9)
Green Lane Primary Academy, Middlesbrough

Magical Toyshop

As the sun descended, the misty air grew. Something strange happened in the reclusive toyshop. Something had been knocking over magical toys that no muggle found out about. Was it the three-eyed-aliens? Or was it Angelina? She is a ballerina. Suddenly, I heard a beautiful harmonious sound. It was coming from the warehouse which had the toys in. Slowly, I walked to the dim lit room. My heart was beating like a drum. I walked through the door. I saw something move. Suddenly, I heard a rattle, It was singing Princess Nella.

Aliya Din (9)
Green Lane Primary Academy, Middlesbrough

Crimson Red Ferrari

It was Christmas Day at 10am when I opened my best and final present. It was my brand new remote-controlled five thousand! It was a crimson red Ferrari! I loved it! I spent the rest of my Christmas Day in the park with my Gran and my Ferrari five thousand. Then, we got an ice cream and I played on the climbing frame. After that, we walked home. Well, we pretty much crawled home, sweating. Me and Gran were so, so tired but then we noticed one tiny problem. Actually, it was a huge problem. Where's the car...?

Jesse Jay French (10)
Green Lane Primary Academy, Middlesbrough

Checkmate

Ben took a step forward and took a step to the right. Suddenly, a white knight boomed, "Stop!" Ben froze. In front of him, he saw the black army of chess pieces. The chess pieces started to move around the board to check the black king. Ben realised he was in danger, he was a pawn in the game. The white bishop moved to protect the white king, but was taken out by the black queen. A pawn captured the queen and then the black king was in checkmate. All the pieces ran to the end of the board.

Thomas Williams (9)

Green Lane Primary Academy, Middlesbrough

Runaway Bear

Once upon a Christmas, Tommy was having a clear out in his bedroom, to make room for his Christmas toys. Barney the bear, that he had since he was a baby, thought he was going to be replaced. When Tommy went downstairs to decorate the tree, Barney thought, *should I run away? No, wait, yes! I'm away?* Barney got out the window and ran to the park. Tommy went upstairs, but Barney wasn't there. He ran to the park and looked everywhere. There he was, Barney the Bear. Tommy was so happy!

Lilly May Davies (9)
Green Lane Primary Academy, Middlesbrough

The New Toy

As the lights went down in the toy store, all the toys sprang to life, they needed to see the beautiful new toy! She had been so popular with all the children that day. They all wanted to play with the Russian ballerina doll that twirled around to beautiful music on her podium. The toys climbed the shelf to meet the new toy, but as they got to her shelf, she was crying. A little girl had broken her, and she was on the defect shelf! She was so upset as she knew she would never be played with again!

Devon Anne Garbutt (10)
Green Lane Primary Academy, Middlesbrough

Monkey

Hello everyone. My name is Monkey. I'm in a chest box in James' playroom and I really want to come out. I have been stuck in this boring, old box for four weeks now. I hate it! At least my friends can easily get me out because they are not in a chest box. Yes! Now I can start playing with them.
I hear footsteps coming upstairs. I quickly go into my old chest box and I am quiet for a moment. James comes in and plays with me. At least, I am out of this, I'm enjoying myself!

Iman Malik (9)
Green Lane Primary Academy, Middlesbrough

Turbo The Tiny Turtle

It was the last couple of days of school when kids and their parents came to Mr Brown's toyshop. One kid called Harry came every day. Harry was on Mr Brown's top customer chart! One day, Harry and his dad went to Mr Brown's shop. Harry looked around for some toys. Suddenly, Harry spotted a small toy, he picked it up. It was a tiny turtle, he bought the turtle and named it Turbo. He took Turbo home. There was a button on Turbo's back. Harry pressed it. It was a turbo boost!

Zakariyya Rafi (9)
Green Lane Primary Academy, Middlesbrough

Lost In The Jungle

All of a sudden, I'm on the ground, confused and wondering where Jack is.
Me, a stuffed bear, lost in what looks like a jungle. In the distance, I see a brown, furry, huge-eyed creature. It starts to swing, then grabs me like a sponge. I begin to feel hopeless! Then Jack comes with a lady. The lady grabs me out of the creature's hands. Jack takes me into his arms and says, "I've missed you! You're safe, thanks to the zookeeper!"
What a hectic day!

Amani Mariam Fardin (10)
Green Lane Primary Academy, Middlesbrough

Boo's Journey To Home!

Thrown away on a train, alone until a lovely girl found me, from that moment onwards, we played together and had so much fun. Bedtimes were the best as I always slept with her until, one Christmas, the worst thing happened. She was gifted with a new teddy. All alone, once again, while she played with her teddy and forgot about me. I ran away. The train had left me in a place that looked like a box, I climbed through the window. It was Heaven. I had met a lot like me. It was a playgroup.

Fatimah Ali (9)
Green Lane Primary Academy, Middlesbrough

My Magical Giraffe

One night, when I was sleeping, I heard something move. I got out of bed to check, there was nothing there, so I went back to bed. It moved again, I turned my light on to check where the noise was coming from. I slowly and carefully took my time to see where it was coming from. I heard that it was coming from under my bed. I climbed back out of bed and bent down to look, and to my amazement and surprise, my toy giraffe had come to life! We became best friends for life.

Ella Armstrong (9)
Green Lane Primary Academy, Middlesbrough

The Cow Toy

When I entered my bedroom, I went to bed. When I go to bed, I never wake up as I am a deep sleeper. As I was sleeping, my Lego figures came to life with all the other toys. They thought I knew that they were real because a cowboy told them I knew they were real. They needed a plan until they found out I didn't know so they needed to catch the cowboy for revenge and take the cowboy on the train. They caught the train and caught the cowboy!

Murtaza Ishfaq (10)
Green Lane Primary Academy, Middlesbrough

Toys Under The Bed

My story is about toys moving in my bedroom. I thought it was my mum.
So I set a trap and stayed awake the whole night. I was hiding under my bed. There was a loud noise and my toys picked me up and carried me down to the basement. The leader of the toys was a robot. They had me tied to a chair, All the toys went out to get some more children to be their prisoners. Whilst they were gone, I was able to escape, so I ran back up to my bedroom.

Robert Dylan Coates (10)
Green Lane Primary Academy, Middlesbrough

Plastic Army

Deep in the dark, wooden box, the plastic army jumped into action.

The Commander shouted, "Men, we have a big job today!"

In the garden, Dad had lost his glasses. General Alex used binoculars. Something sparkled in the sunlight.

"Over here!" he whispered. They all crawled towards the spectacles.

"On the count of three..." came the command.

Running quickly, the army pushed open the cat flap. The rest of the plastic army was waiting on the table. They pulled up the glasses with string.

"Retreat men!" called Commander.

"Oh there's my glasses," said Dad, "I don't remember leaving them there!"

Alex Mark Ludbrook (7)
Keelham Primary School, Bradford

The Amazing Pirate Bedroom

Cole set off to rugby training. His bedroom was silent and very still. Then, something came crashing from the waves, "Argh! Ahoy!" Cole's bedroom was full of water and waves! His toy pirate ship had come to life! *Splash!* The anchor crashed to the bottom of the sea. The pirates were looking for gold, shiny treasure. Captain Blackbeard shouted, "Treasure, I've found the treasure," but then, *stomp, stomp!* Cole was walking upstairs to his bedroom. The toys froze still like statues. When he opened his bedroom door he was cross, his little sister had been playing with his toys again!

Theo-Cole Cyprien (8)
Keelham Primary School, Bradford

Rex's Escape

Max had a ferocious toy spider called Rex, with hairy arms and legs and eyes of the brightest red. One day, Rex escaped the toy box and saw a black cat who heard the pitter-patter of Rex's feet. "Hi," said Rex.
"I'm Molly, let's be friends!" said the cat.
"I'd love to!" Rex replied.
Playing upstairs in Max's bedroom, they made a horrible mess!
When Max heard the noise, he went upstairs and saw Molly with his toy spider.
He was angry! "Grrr!" said Max. "Out!" They were never allowed to play together again...

Zack Charles Elliott (8)
Keelham Primary School, Bradford

Earthquake

While the girl was at school, her tiny Playmobil people at home came to life.

They walked to the toy swimming pool and got their cossies on. There was an earthquake. Everyone was frightened. The baby fell into the water. The mum was terrified and worried about her. The lifeguard was watching them. Her job was making sure that everyone was safe. The lifeguard saw a baby in the water and jumped in to save her. The mum said, "Thank you lifeguard."

The lifeguard said, "You're very welcome." They all rushed back to their places before the girl came home.

Courtney Mannion (8)

Keelham Primary School, Bradford

Night In A Classroom

So Cupcake, Amber and Daisy came together and went to reception and nursery classroom. The children played with the toys all day. Cupcake is a baby, Amber is a toddler and Daisy is a dog. So Cupcake and her friends got a bit poorly. They were poorly because the children were playing with them roughly. When the toys got home, they had a rest and talked about their day at pre-school. "Argh!" screamed Amber.
Suddenly, a big noise was heard by Daisy. Everyone wondered what the matter was. That was weird. No one was there, just Mum's dressing gown!

Radhika Parmar (7)

Keelham Primary School, Bradford

Ollie's Party

"Yes! Finally, she's asleep. I can get all the soldiers together. Toys! Out from under the bed, we're having a party downstairs! We can zip wire down the stairs to the toy ground. Come on, we need to go, soldiers go!"
Off the soldiers went to get things ready. They all zip wired downstairs and started to play. They settled down to have some food.
"After all, we all have had a good time and it's time to go now." The soldiers turned the zip wire into a climbing rope. When they were all up, Lucy was just waking up!

Lucy Jacques
Keelham Primary School, Bradford

Animal Party

One night, whilst I was fast asleep, my toy animals awakened. One monkey swung from my bedpost and landed on my drum kit. He jumped up and down while another monkey found my ukulele. They played some jungle tunes, and the baboons shook their booties. Meanwhile, the giraffe had spotted my cactus on my top shelf. He stretched his neck and nibbled it.

It tickled his long black tongue. The meerkats made some brownies in my kitchen. They decided to share the brownies out with the rest of the animals.

Those animals sure know how to party!

Holden Roberts (8)
Keelham Primary School, Bradford

Michaela And The Funfair Teddy

A funfair came to Michaela's town. Her mum gave her some spending money to go. She saw her favourite stall, the coconut shy. Michaela won a giant teddy!

The fair was closing and Michaela was about to leave when the bear came alive! They hid until everyone had left. Michaela went on all the rides with her teddy and the other toys. When it was time to leave, Teddy was sad. He wanted to stay with all the other toys. Michaela was sad but understood it was okay because they saw each other every year when the fair returned.

Scarlett Ava Simkiss (8)
Keelham Primary School, Bradford

Life As A Football

I'm round and bouncy, I've got patterns on me and I'm white and black in colour. All of a sudden, I'm picked up by a boy and the boy says, "Who wants to play football?" I hear lots of cheering and they put me in the middle of the field. A whistle is blown and suddenly I'm kicked. I fly in the sky and another boy heads me. I'm flung into the goal and the children cheer. I'm again kicked hard and zoom into the sky, one side of the field to the other. Yippee! I'm so happy!

Muhammad Hamzah (7)
Keelham Primary School, Bradford

Unicorn Adventure Shorts

I am Emily's toy unicorn from the pound shop. I am the first ever toy unicorn and I live in her bedroom with all of her other toys and teddies. When Emily is not looking my favourite food is popcorn, chocolate and sweets. I was thinking of just staying in the bedroom, but instead made a portal with my horn and I ended up in Candy Land. Everything was made of chocolate and sweets. The trees were made of green and brown icing. The lake was made of melted chocolate. I decided to eat everything and teleport back home.

Emily Walter (7)
Keelham Primary School, Bradford

Cloudy And Sushi

I have got a toy cat called cloudy and she wakes up at night and plays with my real cat called Sushi. My toy cat is white and fluffy. My toy cat wakes up Sushi who is all grey. They both go downstairs and start running around, knocking things over. Once they have finished making a mess, they both go looking for food. Their favourite food in the whole world is sardines. When Sushi and Cloudy have eaten a mountain of sardines, they both sit down and watch their favourite programme on TV, called 'Tom and Jerry'.

Pearl Roberts (7)
Keelham Primary School, Bradford

The Adventures Of Angry Green Man

Angry Green Man isn't your normal teddy, he doesn't have furry ears or a button nose, he is the cuddliest superhero in my bedroom. He is my best friend and I take him everywhere. He comes with me when I have my breakfast, he comes outside to play and he even goes to Grandma's house.
When I go to sleep he is next to me but when I wake up he is never there.
When I'm asleep he gets up to all sorts of things. Once I woke up and he was eating sweets in my kitchen! That's our secret!

Charlie Michael Carter (8)
Keelham Primary School, Bradford

Toys Who Come Alive

There was a boy who had toys, but he wanted them to come alive. He decided to make a potion. He looked around and collected feathers, sugar and milk.

Then, he stirred it. He put his favourite toys in, but he had to wait a while for the potion to work. Later that day, he heard a funny noise upstairs and wondered if the potion had worked. When he went upstairs, the toys were playing games!

They asked him if he wanted to play. The boy was so happy and could not wait to start adventures with his toys.

Ethan Holroyd (7)

Keelham Primary School, Bradford

Donkey

Hi, I'm Donk, I belong to Tommy. He is funny but a little bit naughty too. When Tommy falls asleep, I go on adventures! Last night, we all got a plane to Fuerteventura. We all met on the beach, Ted and Fred were already there, playing in the sea. All of a sudden, Sharky, Tommy's cuddly shark popped his head out of the waves. We all screamed! Sharky was scared of all the noise!
He quickly swam back to Tommy's bed. I ran as fast as I could to make sure I got back home before Tommy woke up.

Travis Mark Tailford (7)
Keelham Primary School, Bradford

The Diary Of The Toy Cat

Dear Diary, a few weeks ago while playing with choo-choo train and the fluffiest teddy bear everything was awesome until robbers came into our toy store. We were taken. Luckily, I fell out of the bag and was left on the pavement for many days until a dog came and took me as a chewy toy. The dog's owner got home and saw me and fell in love with me, so she washed, dried and fluffed me and will keep me forever. I feel a tingling in my chest. My plastic eyes are real. I am now a real cat!

Lili Runaviciute
Keelham Primary School, Bradford

Woody Saves Buzz!

In a house far away, where people aren't about, the toys come alive but some people don't think that is true, do you? This is how the story begins. When all was calm, the people were out of the house, the toys came alive. When Woody woke up, he couldn't find Buzz anywhere, but downstairs, he saw him. Buzz was broken! His arm was on the window. It was tall! Woody climbed to the window, he got the arm and gave it to Buzz, but then Woody got down and put Buzz's arm back on!

Molly-May Thornton (8)
Keelham Primary School, Bradford

Batty Adventure

One day something strange happened, my teddies were up to something. The bravest teddy went on a quest to find where I go during the day. His name is Batty. For some reason, my bag felt heavier. I didn't realise that he was in my bag. I went to get my lunch and it was gone! I saw breadcrumbs in my bag. I wondered what had happened. I went home hungry. I got home, got my bag and emptied it. He was inside! I got him out and wondered how he'd got in there. I didn't know!

Ellie Drake (8)
Keelham Primary School, Bradford

Ballerina Bear

My name is Annie. I'm a Ballerina Bear and I belong to Bethany. I was bought as a present for Bethany. Before that, I lived in a toyshop where I was lonely and sad as I had no friends. Each night, Bethany would tidy her toys up before bed and we would all lay quiet until we were sure all the family were asleep.

Then, me and the rest of the toys would all climb out of the box and play together in the wardrobe and that made me very happy.

Bethany Wood (8)
Keelham Primary School, Bradford

The Dark Night

"Lucy!" said Katie. "Rebecca's gone!"

"Yes," said Lucy.

"It's time to have some fun, alright?" said Tom, turning on the music.

"No!" said Lucy, "that's not what I meant!"

"Then what did you mean?"

"She meant revenge! Let's prank!"

"Yes, that's a good idea! Let's put blue food colouring on her toothbrush, then, when she brushes her teeth, they will go blue! Then, she'll think that we are cursed and she will take us to a charity shop! From the charity shop, we will escape and then, we will finally be free!"

"Yes!"

Ayesha Sheraz (9)
Mill Lane Junior Infant & Early Years School, Batley

The Creepy Doll And Her Owner

In a haunted house, there lived a girl called Daisy. One day, Daisy found a doll. The doll looked innocent, but was it?

Daisy disrespected Annabelle because she dragged her around the house, she used to turn her upside down and carried Annabelle by her leg.

"No!" said Annabelle. "I can't take this."

Years later, some people moved in and they saw Annabelle.

"Who is crying," asked a lady called Sophie.

"I don't know," said a man called Tommy.

They looked upstairs and it was Annabelle. They asked, "Why are you crying?"

Annabelle said, "None of your business!"

Zara Ali (10)

Mill Lane Junior Infant & Early Years School, Batley

The Broken Necklace

Every time when Libby goes to school, the toys always play with Libby's new things. One day, Horsy, a toy horse, found something, something that was shiny. Horsy told the other toys to come over here, "What's that?" asked Piggy.
"That's a necklace!" explained Octo. The toys thought it was a new toy, but it wasn't a new toy. It was Libby's new necklace. Octo tried to tell the others it wasn't a new toy. Piggy accidentally dropped the necklace. They stood there in horror.
"Libby will be shocked!" said Octo.
"What should we do?" asked Piggy.

Adetutu Eniola (11)
Mill Lane Junior Infant & Early Years School, Batley

Pogba And His Four Friends

One day in a lovely toyshop called Toys 'R' Us, there were three toys called Pogba, Tom and Tomy. They loved playing cricket. There was a girl called Annabelle. She loved toys. She bought the three toys and as she got home, she started putting make-up on them. They didn't like it, so they tried running away, but she caught them. Then, one day, Annabelle went to her cousin's house and forgot about them, so they played cricket. Then, they heard Annabelle opening the door, so they jumped out the window, and went back to their lovely shop called Toys 'R' Us.

Rumaan Anwary (11)
Mill Lane Junior Infant & Early Years School, Batley

The Invisible Doll

Once, there lived a young, peculiar girl named Lilly. Everyone made fun of her in school, especially Tom Watson. She had old, silver braces; two short pigtails hanging down from her ears and glasses that were too big for her face.

After school, she would normally go shopping with her Aunt Jennifer. As soon as they entered the shopping mall, there was a huge doll that she adored, so she bought it. The night rapidly approached, and Lilly slept with the doll. All of a sudden, it disappeared. It appeared on the rusty rocking chair, swinging. It moved closer...

Haniyah Maqbool (10)
Mill Lane Junior Infant & Early Years School, Batley

Sophie And The Knock Out

Far, far away, there lived a little girl named Sophie. Sophie was three foot tall and was in Year 6. She was the smallest in the school.

One day, Sophie went to school and everybody made fun of her, especially a boy called Jake Paul. Jake Paul always stole her lunch money, pulled her hair and always poked her.

One afternoon, Sophie brought her toy to school, and Jake Paul stole her lunch money, so the toy chased Jake Paul and got it back.

Jake Paul was stuck in hospital because his face was crushed. Sophie's toy felt guilty.

Jabeer Mohammed (10)

Mill Lane Junior Infant & Early Years School, Batley

The Football Game

One dark, stormy night some toys had a game of football, when Ben and Dom were eating their tea. Then they heard a bang!

"What was that?" said Ben.

"I don't know," said Dom.

The toys wanted to finish the game before Ben and Dom came to their room.

The next day, when Ben and Dom were at school, the toys continued their game before they got played with. They didn't like being played with, they wished they had better owners than Ben and Dom. Then, they had an amazing plan. Revenge!

Dominic Powles (10)
Mill Lane Junior Infant & Early Years School, Batley

Dolly's Day Out

Life was amazing! Unicorn wallpaper covered the walls. Trophies clothed the bare shelves with pride. But the most prized possession was the crimson toy box filled with all the best toys. Any toy who had the distinct honour to be in the toy box must be very special. Lucy lived underneath the bed. It wasn't a half bad life for a dolly. She thought the toy box was overrated. She loved waking up to the alarm ringing, shortly followed by the unique sound of the owner moaning! But today, something was different. Four walls trapped Lucy...

Zulaika Laher (10)
Mill Lane Junior Infant & Early Years School, Batley

Lucy's Amazing Adventure

One summer day, there was a girl called Lucy and she was excited. There was a school fair! She loved school fairs because she could get teddies and she loved them.

It was the school fair, Lucy ran to the teddies first. She saw one that was magnificent. She really wanted it. Her mum said, "You can get it!"

After that, she put her teddy on a bench and went to get some candyfloss. When she looked, her teddy was gone. She cried all night.

The next morning, she found her teddy on the floor and she was so happy.

Aleeza Khan (11)

Mill Lane Junior Infant & Early Years School, Batley

Lost And Found

"Welcome to Liontastic Land, where there are special offers on toys! Come, play whack-a-toy and win a lion," said the man named Matthew. Toby followed the instructions and won a lion. That was always his dream toy! He was overwhelmed with joy. Toby was jumping around with his mum, and all that excitement made him put down his toy and forget all about it. Tracy, a little girl, picked up the toy and walked off in search of the owner. All of a sudden, her mum was gone. Tracy and Matthew found her together near the duck station.

Zara Mahmood (11)
Mill Lane Junior Infant & Early Years School, Batley

The Killer Robot

One morning, Harry's parents came to his room and gave him a new toy. He quickly opened his present. Harry was amazed. It was a robot! The robot charged around the room. Harry grabbed the robot and laid it on the bed. The robot had red eyes and an angry face. The robot whispered, "You will die!" The robot shot the window in anger. It was almost night and the robot was acting like a maniac. He was shooting down buildings and was killing toys. It was a black sky, and the robot shouted, "You will all bow down!"

Huzaifah Seedat (10)

Mill Lane Junior Infant & Early Years School, Batley

The Disaster!

Once there was a toy dog called Layla. She was playing with her friends Rex and Ellie. Layla jumped and caught her leg, fluff was flying everywhere. "Oops!" What was Daisy going to say? They heard Daisy coming, so they got into the toy box and found themselves in a different world. It was a teddy bear hospital, where she could get her leg fixed! After she got it fixed, she met some new friends, Lilly, Chloe and Bob. Sadly, they had to say bye! Daisy picked up Layla and hugged her. She then ended up in the charity pile...

Codi Slocombe (10)
Mill Lane Junior Infant & Early Years School, Batley

Whisker's Adventure

24th November 2017

Dear Diary, my heart sank when Mum said that all the teddies had to go. She yanked me out of the toy box, and put me on the charity shop pile! I felt bad for the teddies who got thrown on the garbage pile! I was in the corner of the charity shop, when Bob the Builder said, "You will never get an owner."

Peppa Pig said, "You will never be popular."

Just after that, a woman picked me up, threw me in the car and that's how I ended up in this nursery.

Jorja Bedford (10)

Mill Lane Junior Infant & Early Years School, Batley

Rex's Revenge

Once upon a time, there was a three-year-old girl called Lucy. Lucy loved one of her teddy's. She called him Rex.

Rex was a living toy who had a terrible life to go through. The moment when Lucy steps out of her room, Rex gathers his crew. He wanted revenge because Lucy always holds him by his leg, she gives him wet kisses and gives him tight hugs. Disgusting!

One day, Lucy went downstairs to have dinner. Rex and his crew looked around her room to find a shock pen. Fortunately, they found one...

Hafsa Hussain (10)
Mill Lane Junior Infant & Early Years School, Batley

Woody's Haunting Night

One dark, stormy night Woody, Buzz and Jessie woke up in a strange place, a haunted house. Woody explored the house and then Jessie screamed, "Argh!"
Then, Buzz ran to save the day, but there was nothing there. Creepy! Suddenly, Woody ended up in a maze. The instructions were, 'You have one life, so use it wisely. There will be dangerous obstacles along the way.' Woody jumped over some obstacles running away from some beasts and somehow, Woody spotted the exit and he escaped. Lucky Woody!

Evie-Mai Gott (9)
Mill Lane Junior Infant & Early Years School, Batley

Maya And House

Once upon a time, there was this little girl called Maya. She loved to play with her toy house. She was always looking after it, making sure everything stayed perfectly. She kept the green children playing in a green park and she kept all the pink people together. It was a sweet and perfect little world. Maya wished that one day she could live in a world like this.

One day, Maya woke up in a wonderland. Everything she imagined about the toy house had come true. She was very happy and very surprised.

Zainab Mahmood (10)
Mill Lane Junior Infant & Early Years School, Batley

The Dark Knight

In a land far away, lived a boy who had a fringe too big for his face. His name was Tom. Tom's name had lots of meanings, but one in particular, dumb!
So as dumb as Tom was, he said yes to everything. It was no surprise when Mark, Tom's friend asked him if he wanted to go to a castle.
The next morning, they went and as they stepped into the castle, Tom felt an eerie chill on his spine. As they entered into another room, a dark mist formed into a toy knight and headed towards them...

Salma Hussain (9)
Mill Lane Junior Infant & Early Years School, Batley

Untitled

One stormy night, an evil Zurg was imprisoned against his wishes in the Forest of Doom. When he had managed to find his way out of the forest, he saw Woody. When he saw Woody, he instantly felt the urge to fight him, even though Woody had a big advantage! Suddenly, Woody smiled, then he blasted Zurg with thunder but it had the opposite effect than what Woody had expected.
Suddenly, Zurg blasted Woody with all his power that he gained from the blast of thunder and blasted it at Woody. Woody died.

Kaif Zanfar (10)

Mill Lane Junior Infant & Early Years School, Batley

Katie In The Woods

Once upon a time, there was a little girl called Katie. She went for a walk in the woods and she saw her friends playing together. Katie just ignored her friends and went on the other side. Katie heard a crying noise from the woods.

It was a scary toy. Katie ran home to show what she'd found in the woods.

She called her friends to come over to her house. On Saturday, Katie's friends came over at 9am. The next day, they all went for a walk in the woods and played hide-and-seek.

Selina Ashiq (10)

Mill Lane Junior Infant & Early Years School, Batley

The Disappearance

Lola was coming home from school when she noticed a toy rabbit up for sale in Rabbitville. Immediately, she told her mother to buy it for her, and in an instant, it was in her arms. When she reached home, she thought of a name, he was named Mr Jingles. Soon, night fell and Lola fell asleep, Jingles by her side.

His tender and soft feel comforting her. The sun rose up high in the sky, feeling proud. Lola woke up and had a big stretch. She looked over to her side, but he wasn't there!

Umaimah Hussain (10)
Mill Lane Junior Infant & Early Years School, Batley

The Escape

Once upon a time, there was a mean and awful boy called Alex. He was four.

He always treated his toys awfully. He would throw his toys around and rip them.

One day, a toy called Rex decided to run away when Alex went to school.

All of the other toys agreed to run away.

The next day, they tried to run away. They saw Mum making Alex his breakfast. They sneaked past Mum and escaped through the back door!

Fahad Raja (10)
Mill Lane Junior Infant & Early Years School, Batley

The Toy Murderer

Josh was an ordinary robot who was played with a lot. He was almost played with every day. He also had accessories like a shield and guns.
One day, his owner took him to the park, but suddenly, Josh turned evil! Josh put his accessories on and fired his gun at his owner, and one of the bullets went through his owner's hand. The owner fought Josh and then he picked him up and went home and put Josh in the scrapyard.

Nathan Wagner (10)
Mill Lane Junior Infant & Early Years School, Batley

Rosie's Bedroom

"Be good teddies," instructed Rosie, as she slammed the door shut.

"Coast is clear," whispered Unicorn.

"Let's have a dance party!" shouted Dolly.

The toy radio turned the music on and everyone got in the middle of the room and danced like mad.

"Let's play musical statues!" chirped the toy soldier, "because I am the best at it!"

Jelly legs didn't like the thought of that.

"Shouldn't we keep an eye out for Rosie?" sighed the toy clock.

"Yes," replied Unicorn.

The toy clock shouted, "She's coming." Everyone dropped on the floor.

Rosie entered the room, looking very confused.

Daisy Snowden
Totley All Saints CE Primary School, Sheffield

The Glontosaurus

"Attack the obese creature, which is covered in green slime... now!" screeched the powerful toy general. The gloopy Glontosaurus bounced on top of the pale, fearless toy soldiers of Zermincraft, as soon as a flicker of light shone from the scruffy, dingy curtains, all Zermincraft soldiers were now part of the catastrophic monster! A waif-like orphan child entered the room, as she looked up she spotted the walls oozing with thick, gloopy, jelly-like slime. While calling the matron Valentina got the turbo vacuum and started sucking up the monster.
She succeeded in defeating her enemy.

Lily Hope Naylor (11)
Totley All Saints CE Primary School, Sheffield

Teddy Trouble

Stomp! Stomp! "It's coming! Battle stations everyone!" yelled Chief Louie.

Then, there came a deafening roar and the boy, Teddy Bot 2000, came into view.

"Fire!" Hundreds of bullets came out of their guns, but the Teddy Bot jumped over and headed towards Louie. "Help me!" But the bear's foot came down and suddenly a massive light appeared in the room.

All of the soldiers turned to see a figure loom over them and then they all fell over into a massive heap. "I thought I put you away?" said the boy, and left the room.

Aron King (11)
Totley All Saints CE Primary School, Sheffield

Crock Cave!

Once there was a toy that was passed down from generations of the Smith Family. Each person who owned it always swore it was magic...
"Today is the day I adventure out to seek the mysteries of Crock Cave!" said the dog.
Ten minutes later, they arrived at Crock Cave and adventured in. What mysteries would await him? Gold? Silver? Just then, a loud roar came from outside the cave. "Tiger!" screamed the dog. He ran to the other side of the cave and escaped through a crack. He arrived home safely and crept back in his toy box...

Jessica Smith (11)
Totley All Saints CE Primary School, Sheffield

The Beautiful Beach

Toy had the most fantastic dream of her life. She was at the bright, beautiful, sunny beach and it was absolutely miraculous. It had an ice cream van that was luminous and the stickers on the window smelt exactly like the ice cream flavours they sold. On top of the cliffs, the view was spectacular, like nothing you would ever see. You could see the calm sea gently leaning onto the lonely, peaceful shore, which would've made you want to leap like a frog into the shimmering sapphire-blue waters. Toy woke up to see the beach next to her!

Lily Pearl Flint (11)
Totley All Saints CE Primary School, Sheffield

Trapped!

For years, I have been stuck on a dusty shelf, feeling no emotions apart from afraid and trapped! But yesterday I escaped from that wretched toyshop. My first move was at 11.30pm I climbed up on to the windowsill. Luckily, the window was opened a crack, so I grabbed my chance and jumped out.
When I got outside, I knew it was a great decision! There were people and moving slabs of metal everywhere. It has been two months now, and I am loving life! Even though I am living in a dustbin, I no longer feel trapped.

Rafi Jack Day (11)
Totley All Saints CE Primary School, Sheffield

Sam The Train!

One day, in a far away town, lived a beautiful toy train named Sam. Sam the train saved the day by rescuing Fred, the toy horse. Fred the horse had been stuck on a train track. After rescuing Fred the horse, they went on a camping trip to celebrate. "Thank you for saving me, Sam!" exclaimed Fred. That night, they had a small campfire and toasted marshmallows. "These marshmallows looks tasty!" But before he could eat it, Fred gobbled it up! They both laughed. They both had a wonderful time and were best friends forever!

Kyle Hanson (10)
Woodley SEN School & College, Huddersfield

Tomb Raider

On a planet called Glorb Norb, there was a toy gun war. Poorie, a toy alien, was fighting Tomb Raider with a laser sword, Poorie got shot and stabbed. The robot Tomb Raider got shot, but magically rebuilt itself. Poorie escaped and Tomb Raider was on the hunt to find him and put in jail. "Uh, uh, uh!" said Poorie as his warning to Tomb Raider, so Tomb Raider failed in finding him, but a rocket arrived at Glorb Norb and took Tomb Raider safely back to Earth, leaving Poorie to take control over Glorb Norb.

Logan Watt (11)
Woodley SEN School & College, Huddersfield

Santa Deserves A Present

Once upon a time, Julie the little pig went to Smyths toyshop. She went to buy trains. The shop was very busy. She had to wait in queues to order the train. She got enough money to buy the trains and took them home. Julie was really excited! She bought the train set as a Christmas Present for Santa. She wrapped the present in sparkly green paper and sent it to Santa. She put the present under the Christmas tree, so Santa will come through the chimney and take his beautiful present.

Tyler O'Donnell (10)
Woodley SEN School & College, Huddersfield

Little Brick's Adventure

One stormy night there was a brick, a Lego brick. It was lost and could not find the set it belonged to. He was sad. Meanwhile, a boy called Tim was looking for a piece that was not in the set he had. He was sad! Back to the main character, Brick found the house. He felt a lot happier when he walked through the door and saw the Lego complete builds on the walls. He went upstairs into a room of a crying boy, then the boy looked up and picked the piece up.

Charlie Green (12)
Woodley SEN School & College, Huddersfield

Iron Man Gets A New Suit

We need to build ourselves a toy Iron Man suit. First, we need to build the leg and then we do the other leg. We will make it out of super strong plastic that has really powerful metal inside. The chest is made of the same material, but it can help you to breathe underwater. The helmet has flowing blue eyes which makes the suit really awesome. The arms are really powerful and there is a gloved left hand, to help defeat all of the enemies.

Thomas Dunning (12)
Woodley SEN School & College, Huddersfield

The Great Day Out

One day in 1988, the toy bus goes out and about. A few hours later, he arrives in the small town of Whitby. Although he arrives at Arriva North East bus depot, he is not welcome. So he sets off for home, to Newcastle.

There, after five hours of traffic jams, he finds his home. After a very tiring day, he arrives in Newcastle and goes to sleep after a well-earned rest.

Max Jagger (12)
Woodley SEN School & College, Huddersfield

Toy Car And The Beach Adventure

On a hot sunny day, Toy Car went to the beach. He wanted to enter a sand race track competition. He went to the race start and his engine was fast. He felt happy. Toy Car could see the finish line. He zoomed forward with all the other fast cars. Toy Car saw a big wave coming from the sea. The wave got Toy Car and he was swept out to sea!

Rudie Hughes (12)
Woodley SEN School & College, Huddersfield

Cars

There was a very fast toy car, whose name was Speed. Speed was racing his friends on the race track. Speed had lots of colours all over his body. His friends accidentally crashed their cars. Speed went to save his friends, when he saved his friends, his car changed his colours.

Brandon Johnson (12)
Woodley SEN School & College, Huddersfield